CW00529944

FIVE POP BALLADS

FOR SSA CHOIR WITH

PIANO ACCOMPANIMENT

Novello Publishing Limited
14/15 Berners Street, London W1T 3LJ

Cover design by Miranda Harvey
Printed in the United Kingdom by Caligraving Limited, Thetford, Norfolk

California Dreamin'

Words & Music by **John Phillips & Michelle Gilliam**
Arranged by **Milt Rogers**
(Piano with optional string bass, guitar and percussion)

4

he knows I'm gon - na stay.___

he knows I'm gon - na stay.___

stay.

Cal - i - for - nia

A7sus4

A7

Cal - i - for - nia dream - in' on such a win-ter's day.___

Cal - i - for - nia dream - in' on such a win-ter's day.___

dream-in'___ on such a win-ter's day.___

Dm   C   Bb   C   A7sus4

Imagine

Words & Music by **John Lennon**
Arranged by **Chuck Cassey**

Im-ag-ine there's no heav - en

Im-ag-ine all the peo – ple liv-ing for to-day—

— ah _____ Im-ag-ine there's no coun-tries

— Oh _____

— ah _____ Im-ag-ine there's no coun-tries

Im-ag-ine all the peo - ple liv-ing life in peace__

Im-ag-ine all the peo - ple liv-ing life in peace__

Im-ag-ine all the peo - ple liv-ing life in peace__

Gm/D Cm7 Eb/Bb F Bb/F

— you, you may say__ I'm a __

— you, you may say__ I'm a __

— you

F7 Eb F

join us ___ and the world ___ will be as one.___

join us and the world ___ will be as one.___

join us and the world ___ will be as one.___

Bb Bbmaj7 D D7   Eb   F   Bb   Bb7/Ab G7

f more emphatically

Im-ag-ine no pos-ses-sions   I won-der if you   can___

f more emphatically

Im-ag-ine no pos-ses-sions   I won-der if you   can___

f more emphatically

Im-ag-ine no pos-ses-sions   I won-der if you   can___

f more emphatically
C   Cmaj7   F   C   Cmaj7

no need for greed   or hun - ger

no need for greed   or hun - ger

no need for greed   or hun - ger

F   C   Cmaj7   F

a broth-er-hood of   man _____   Im-ag-ine all   the peo-

a broth-er-hood of   man __   Im-ag-ine all   the peo-

a broth-er-hood of   man __   Im-ag-ine all   the peo-

C   Cmaj7   F   Am/E

-ple, im-ag-ine peo-ple shar-ing all the world__ Oh_____

-ple, im-ag-ine peo-ple shar-ing all the world__ Oh_____

-ple, im-ag-ine peo-ple shar-ing all the world__ Oh_____

Dm7   F/C   G   C/G   G7   *ff*

you may say____ I'm a__ dream-er, dream-er

you may say____ I'm a__ dream-er, dream-er

you may say I'm a

F   G   Am/C   E   E7

but I'm not the on - ly one ___

but I'm not the on - ly one ___

dream - er ___ but I'm not the on - ly one ___

F   G   C   E   E7

I hope some day ___ you'll join us ___

I hope some day you'll join us

___ I hope some day you'll join us

F   G   C   Cmaj7   E   E7

Bridge Over Troubled Water

Words & Music by **Paul Simon**
Arranged by **Clyde Sechler***

Trou-bled Wa - ter   I will lay me down.

When you're down and out,   When you're on the street,

Annie's Song

Words & Music by **John Denver**
Arranged by **Frank Metis**
(With optional rhythm guitar and bass)

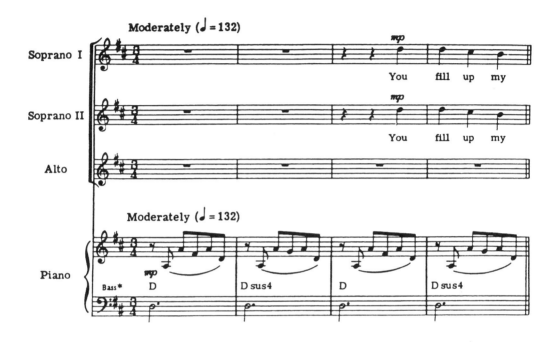

* Bass play L.H. of Piano an octave higher.

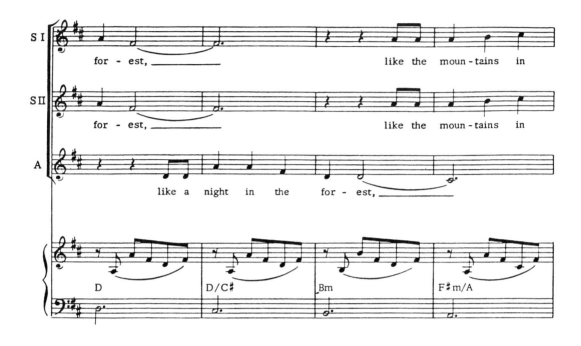

34

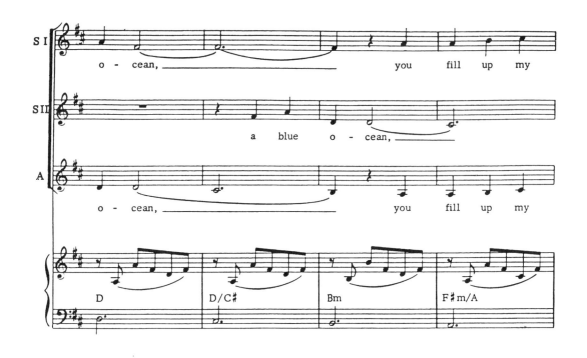

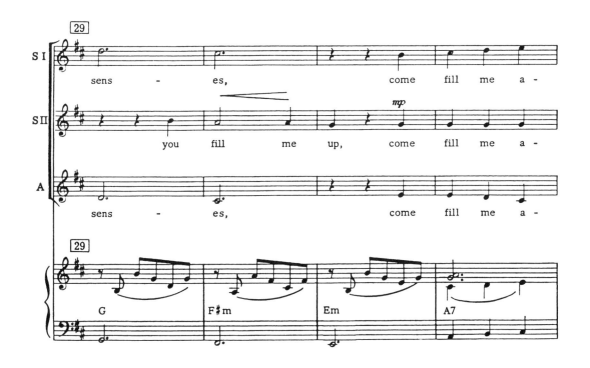

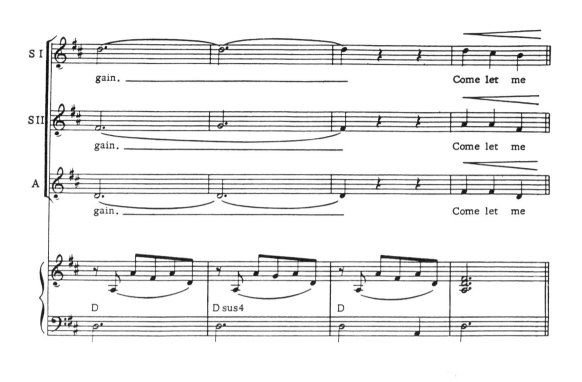

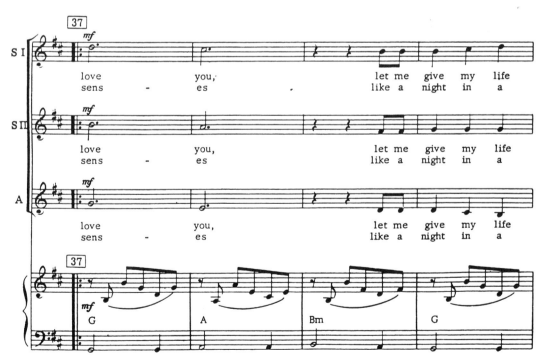

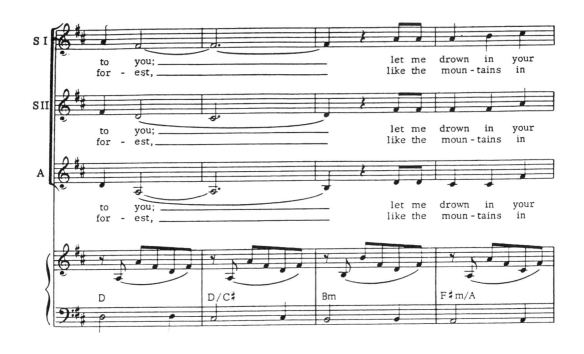

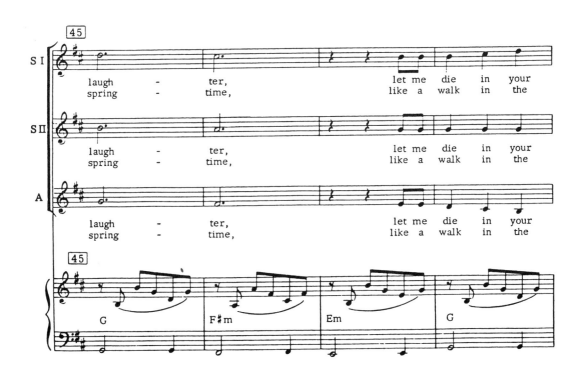

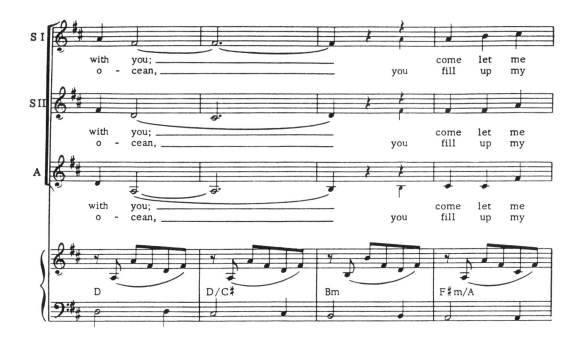

Let It Be

Words & Music by **John Lennon & Paul McCartney**

Shine un-til to-mor-row, let it be._____ I

Shine un-til to-mor-row, let it be, oh let it be. I

Shine un-til to-mor-row, let it be, oh let it be. I

(G)   (D)   (C)   (Bm) (Am) (G)

Melody

wake up to the sound of mu-sic, Moth-er Ma-ry comes to me

wake up to the sound of mu-sic, Moth-er Ma-ry comes to me

wake up to the sound of mu-sic, Moth-er Ma-ry comes to me ___

(D)   (Em)   (D6) (C)